Also by Seth Edgarde

Hart Island
The Devil Speaks Hungarian
Blood Sunrise
St. Louis Blues
Tickleton Abbey
Brick City Blues
Lumina
Lady of the Lake
Ironbound

Short-term Parking

65 Micro Stories

SETH EDGARDE

BLACKBIRD BOOKS
NEW YORK • LOS ANGELES

A Blackbird Original, October 2023

Copyright © 2023 by Seth Edgarde
All rights reserved.

Manufactured in the United States of America.

The events and characters depicted
in this book are fictional.

Cataloging-in-Publication Data

Edgarde, Seth.
Short-term parking: 65 micro stories / Seth Edgarde.
p. cm.
I. Title.
PS3605.D4564 S56 2023 813'.6—dc23 2023946429

Blackbird Books
www.bbirdbooks.com
email us at editor@bbirdbooks.com

ISBN 978-1-61053-026-2

First Edition

10 9 8 7 6 5 4 3 2 1

To cosmic surprises

Contents

Anzio 2 • The Joralemon Street Tunnel 4 • The Party 6 • Late 8 • Snow 10 • Traffic Cop 12 • Voyager 14 • Secret Agent Man 16 • Cold Party Girl 18 • Rive Gauche 20 • Bronze Goddess 22 • Golden Hawk 24 • Clausus Belli 25 • Accident 26 • The Sandwich 28 • Coma 30 • The Cross 32 • Fuck You, You Fucking Fucks! and Other Tales of Old New York 34 • Farting in an Elevator while Pregnant 36 • The Poem 38 • Aspergum Junkie 40 • Bridge and Tunnel 42 • Friends 44 • Pallbearer 45 • The Purple Skoda of Prague 46 • City Island 48 • Pirates 50 • The Girl in the Green Velvet Dress 51 • Opposites 52 • The Tuchis Monster 54 • Amores 56 • Blueberries for Salvatore 58 • Pass / Fail 60 • The Violin Maker 62 •

Peace on Earth or That Time I Made My Fourth Grade Music Teacher Cry 64 • The Yearbook 66 • Closed Casket 68 • Reading Dynamics 70 • Dammit Janet 72 • We Hardly Knew Ye 74 • Pigs in a Blanket 76 • Dead for a Long, Long Time 78 • Meeting Mary Poppins 80 • The Smell of the Desert 82 • Kamikaze 84 • Wrinkles 86 • Marian, the Librarian 88 • L.A. Story 90 • Green Mountains 92 • Warriors 94 • The Old Man and the C 96 • Long-term Parking 98 • The Kids' Table 100 • Cannibals 102 • Jewfro 104 • Paradise on a Razor's Edge 106 • To Live and Die in L.A. 108 • Bottom of the Harbor 110 • The River God 112 • In the Act 114 • Working Girl 116 • Water's Edge 118 • Key West 120 • Desert Rose 122 • Coke and Ice 124

Short-term Parking

Anzio

I can still see my father's hands, even now. I can feel the way my hands wrapped around each of his individual fingers. When he would lift me onto his shoulders, he would wrap them around my ankles. I felt like a giant.

I would grab his thick black hair and giggle. I could feel the indentation where they had inserted the steel plate. I used to press my fingers into the scar. He didn't seem to mind.

During long walks on the California beach, I would hold my arms out.

"Look daddy! I'm an airplane!"

He would tilt his head back and look up at me, riding high. Then, he would crouch low and run around the beach, banking steeply, left and right, as he made the buzzing noise of the propeller, complete with Doppler Effect.

I could see his footprints in the sand as we circled back for another run.

I walk, now, on an empty Mediterranean beach. I take out a picture. My dad is in the middle. His head is covered by a round steel helmet. His hands clutch an M-1 Carbine. He is very young and unshaven and weary, but his eyes still smile out at me.

I put the picture away and turn into the wind. I hear a propeller buzzing as I open the urn and launch my father into flight over the soft Italian beach.

The Joralemon Street Tunnel

I see him every day, even though we have never spoken a word. He is thin but upright, with a smoke-cured face. His dense white hair is slicked back and bright against his dark grey suit.

We both get on the number four train at Joralemon Street at eight fifteen, heading to Wall Street. He is never late. Neither am I.

On this day, as we push into the subway car, through the flow of people, there is an empty seat, like a five dollar bill lying on the ground, unnoticed. He and I go for it at the same time. We look at each other. He gives a polite but awkward smile and extends his lumpy hand, in an elegant gesture.

"Go ahead."

I wave him off.

"No, you take it."

He bows his head with relief and sits.

"Thank you."

The ride through the tunnel under the East River is more jolting than usual. The lights go on and off and then stay off, as the subway car jerks from side to side. I hold the greasy strap and feel my Oxfords creak as I steady myself.

As we gallop over seams between rails, we pass the green light in the tunnel. It shines through the darkness and glows, momentarily, off of his face, as it turns to red. The blackness resumes.

The train slows, as it ascends from under the river's bottom to the station in Lower Manhattan.

He is sitting, slumped, dead in his seat.

The Party

Warm water rushed over my face. I opened my eyes and stared at the stalactites on the shower head. I smelled clean water with a hint of mildew.

"Hey, hurry up! We're going to be late for the party."

I turned off the water and buried my face in a soft, white towel.

The bathroom door opened.

We looked at each other in the mirror.

She was wearing a black and white billowy dress that came down to her knee. Her hair was pulled back off of her freshly made-up face.

I stood, wet and naked.

I grinned at her.

She fought back a smile.

She looked at the antique rose gold Omega that I had bought her for her twenty-seventh birthday.

"You know, we're supposed to be there in less than an hour."

I pulled back the door, and we stood, face-to-face.

"Relax. We've got plenty of time."

I gave her a mischievous look.

I stepped towards her, took her face in my hands, and kissed her Red-Red-Rouge lips.

"No, no, no."

I could taste the dust of Clinique on her face. She savored one last kiss, as she pulled back.

Her dark eyes looked at me as she teetered.

She put her hand to my face and wiped off the lipstick.

We were an hour late. I don't know if anyone noticed.

Late

She wants to stay in, but he's hungry. As they walk to the diner, she feels the bitter wind creep up her skirt, and she reaches for his hand. He resists.

"It's too cold," he says, nestling his fingers deep in his coat pockets.

She thinks about how he used to touch her, grabbing her ass and pulling himself into her. She could smell his saliva as she disappeared underneath him. The next day, she would feel him oozing out from between her legs. It was wet and warm and uncomfortable, but it made her smile.

They take a booth at the diner and order. He has a burger, rare. She has a salad.

While they eat, a pretty girl in tight jeans walks over to the counter. She watches his eyes follow her back pockets all the way to their place on the stool.

As he devours his hamburger, he imagines what it would be like to press himself into her.

He pays the bill, and they put on their coats and leave. He steals one last glance at the pockets on the stool. Her eyes burn from the cold.

Later, back at their apartment, she stands in front of the bathroom sink, in her pajamas, brushing her teeth. She listens to him sleep with deep, meaty breaths, as he dreams of round-assed girls and dancing pockets. She makes up their shopping list for the next day in her head. *Tight jeans. That's what I need.*

Snow

I can still imagine pulling my clothes off and running across the quad naked in the snow. It's been thirteen years, but I still remember the way the fresh New England snow crunched underneath my bare feet, and how pink Scott McGee's skin was, and how different Jen Randall looked without any clothes. It was just the three of us, a college prank—skinny dipping, New England Style, under the moonlight, in the middle of a long winter's night— good clean fun.

The Dean got wind of it and was furious—or at least he pretended to be. He threatened to expel the students who had pulled the stunt, if he ever caught them. I pretended to be concerned and had a secret meeting with Jen. We ended up at the movies, laughing. I wanted to put my arm around her, but I never did.

The snow melted, and I took my exams. I got a summer job in Boston then a permanent job in New York. I thought about going back to school for an MBA, but then I got a big promotion, and my girlfriend didn't want me to go.

I heard that Scott was married with two daughters, one of them autistic. I thought of him as a boy, smiling, naked on the quad, with pink cheeks and a wool hat.

I haven't seen or heard from Jen since graduation, but I think about her and the way she laughed whenever fresh snow blankets the winter ground.

Traffic Cop

I could smell the coffee on his breath.

"Do you know why you've been stopped, sir?" he said.

I could see the red and blue strobe blasting out of the corner of my eye.

"Um. I'm not really sure," I replied.

I noticed his name tag: DAVOS. I wondered what his first name was. Maybe it was Dave. Dave Davos. I smiled.

He took my license and registration. I watched him walk all the way back to his motorcycle.

He was straight and stiff, with a barrel chest and the beginnings of a middle-aged paunch. He was about five foot ten, with a perfectly-groomed, bushy, sandy moustache.

He was otherwise clean-shaven. His hair was graying blond, cropped almost to the scalp. The top of his head hadn't seen a strand in a long time. He wore a wedding ring.

There were two stripes on the sleeve of his blue cop suit. I wasn't sure what that meant, but it didn't seem like enough for a man his age. Maybe he roughed up a suspect and got demoted. Maybe they just didn't like the name Dave Davos.

He handed me my ticket and told me to drive carefully. He actually seemed to mean it, and I thanked him.

Months later, with even traffic school a dim memory, I saw on the news that a motorcycle cop had been killed on a routine traffic stop. They showed him, smiling, with his wife and kids. His first name wasn't Dave.

Voyager

You and I build a Viking boat and sail the Indian Ocean. You slay a two-headed sea serpent off the coast of Madagascar, but in the tussle, you knock over a cushion with your foot.

"All hands aboard! We're taking on water!"

You leave the boat to make repairs while I hold your hand to keep the currents from taking you away. You fight off a shark, climbing back onboard in the nick of time.

"You kids be careful of that coffee table!"

You look at me, face frozen in a mischievous smile.

Dinner is ready, and you ask if I can stay.

You know that I want to and that my dad will say yes. But you can see that I feel bad about leaving him alone. You ask if my dad can come over too.

Forty years from now, you will have gaunt cheeks and rubbery yellow skin, but you will still cover my eyes when you see me staring at the sun, and you will still give me that same smile.

Secret Agent Man

One night I dreamt I was a secret agent for God. He gave me a black briefcase with maps and plans that I couldn't read. My mother was right, I should have paid attention in Hebrew school.

"Excuse me, sir, um, I can't read this."

"You should have paid attention in Hebrew school," he said.

"I know. My mother told me," I replied. I couldn't help but stare. He was only about 5'6 and clean-shaven. He had good hair.

"What, you were expecting maybe John Travolta?"

"How did you know— Oh yeah, I forgot."

I looked down at the briefcase and then back up sheepishly.

"Right. The language." He looked at me. He had dark eyes that exuded confidence. "Just bring it to the tie shop on Orchard, off Delancey." He handed me a piece of paper. "Here's the address. It's in English."

His handwriting was terrible.

He looked at me and grinned. "I'm just playing doctor."

I always knew he had a sense of humor.

I fell asleep on the train—and had a dream within a dream—that the briefcase was stolen. The thief left a clue, but that was in Hebrew too.

So I went to the place on Orchard and asked the man to translate. He did, and I found the briefcase, brought it to him, and asked him to translate that too. He told me it had all of the answers, the answers to everything.

He spoke, and I couldn't understand, but it woke me.

Cold Party Girl

She stood outside in her black party dress, bare legs, hugging herself for warmth. The club had only closed a few minutes before, but almost no one was left—just a few stragglers chatting out front. It was colder out than she had expected; she didn't even have a jacket.

More than anything, she wished she were home in her warm bed instead of out on a semi-deserted street in a not-so-great part of town with her car several blocks away in a dark alley. It was after two in the morning, and her options were evaporating. She had forgotten her phone. Then it started to drizzle, and she felt a hit of panic.

A vagrant was closing in—she could smell him—and she moved towards the last few people, now breaking up, by the door. When she got there, only one was left, a young man, about her age, ordinary, non-descript.

"I'm sorry to bother you," she said. "But can you walk me to my car?"

"Yeah, of course."

He even gave her his jacket.

When they got there, she had the instinct to hug him, but she didn't. "Goodnight" was all she could manage, and he responded in kind, finally breaking a smile that warmed her and filled her with regret at the same time.

Later, safe at home, teeth brushed, getting into her bed in her pajamas, she thought of him. He was nothing to look at, but that smile . . . and she cried.

Rive Gauche

I grew up on the left bank of New York Harbor. Rive Gauche—very gauche—as I liked to call it. New Jersey to the rest of the world. The water was dirty and had a smell to it, especially in the summer, when the mud emerged from the harbor's bottom at low-tide.

Whenever we'd hit a ball down there, we'd let it go.

"They found that boy," my mother would say, talking about a kid who drowned at high tide during a bad storm.

I'm not sure if it really happened or if she just wanted to scare me into staying away from the rats and driftwood, nails and needles, but it worked. Even after they cleaned up the shoreline and dumped all the tires and garbage in a Staten Island landfill, I still kept my distance.

Eventually, I moved all the way to L.A.—Rive Even More Gauche. I bought a vintage car and worked on it on the weekends. I found a pick-your-parts junkyard down at the Port of L.A. and would make my way down to see what treasures I could find.

The man who ran the place told me about the gangs down there and a kid they found drowned down by the docks.

"It happens," I told him, thinking about that other kid, real or not, from that other coast, on that other left bank, so far from Paris but so deep in my mind.

Bronze Goddess

She had bronze skin and platinum hair. Her face was hard but beautiful. He watched her through the dancing people and unbearably loud music. Her heavy lips drew on a cigarette, the elbow of the hand holding it was propped up by her opposite hand. She had a pitted face and looked rough, but it was even-toned and did not detract from her striking looks.

Her curves were immaculate, straddling the line between tasteful and pornographic in a snug-fitting knit dress, ending well above her knees and topping boots with an attitude.

Her boyfriend brought her a drink. She smiled and kissed him and then took a sip. He noticed her light pink lipstick as it marked the glass.

She smiled again, took another drink, and put the glass down. She whispered in her boyfriend's ear, as he put his hand on her hip, then she took his hand and led him to the dance floor.

He watched them dance.

He saw her a couple of days later, out on the quad. She was pale, with no makeup, and had dark hair. It was bitter cold. She was wearing a bulky coat and looked plain, but he knew that she was a bronze goddess.

Golden Hawk

"Let's go to Ohio," she said.

I was dead tired. I looked up at her with half a face, one eye still asleep on the pillow.

"Come on. It'll be fun. We can stay at my mom's place."

Her big girl hips spoke through dryer-tight jeans. I pictured them sitting in my gold and white passenger seat, as they had on trips to Atlantic City, Montreal, Saratoga Springs, and Pittsfield.

"Jimmy wants to come too."

Jimmy wants to fuck you, I thought. I could smell the Fresh Scent Downey through the warm, blue, cotton fibers.

"How far is Boston from Ohio?" I asked.

Later, we sat bruised, jeans torn, with my '57 Studebaker grinning at us, upside down on the highway.

Clausus Belli

He was all wrong to play Santa—even a department store Santa. He was Jewish. And skinny. And he hated Christmas. And, unlike most of his middle eastern brethren, he never could grow a decent beard. But there he was, at a mall in New Jersey, red and overstuffed, with a long line of kids, waiting for the evening to end.

He waited to be annoyed, but it never came. Kids did ask for things for themselves, but nothing crazy—a bike, a video game, a new pair of rollerblades. And some asked for others—a new car for their parents, for grandpa to get out of the hospital. And some just wanted to meet Santa. He listened to them all.

The day ended before he expected, and he picked up his paycheck. He needed the money. He thought about them, all of them, and their conversations as he took off his red suit and headed back to his apartment for a night of cereal and TV.

Accident

It's been two years since my accident. I don't remember anything at all about that day and only a few images from my life before: the floral dress my mother wore when she took me to the park as a little boy; my wife on our wedding day; my brother's funeral. The doctors told me I was clinically dead for more than twelve minutes, but I know that isn't true. In fact, the only thing I know for sure is that that twelve minutes is the only truly real time that I have ever really lived in this world.

I'm in a board meeting now. We're going to be selling a new soft drink. It's bright and red, and they're talking about how the color will affect sales. Nobody is paying any attention to me. I'm like a being in another dimension. Looking at the red liquid, I think how dull it is compared to the flowers on my mother's dress, and I have the urge to run to the window and fly out to join her. But I don't.

The secretary passes out cups of the beverage that she tells me is strawberry, when I ask. I gulp mine down, not realizing how thirsty I was. It's better than I thought, and I ask for another, as my mother's dress fades from my memory.

The Sandwich

Samantha carefully placed the second slice of Wonder bread, laden with French's yellow mustard, on top then sliced her sandwich diagonally. Dave stepped through the kitchen door.

"Is that a sandwich?"

"Yeah it's a sandwich. What does it look like?"

She looked down at it, and then back up at Dave. He had been her roommate for three years, and she knew that look. "Do you want half?"

"No, it's your sandwich. You eat it."

She shrugged, picked up a half, and opened her mouth to take a bite.

"What kind of sandwich?"

She stopped, turned to him. "Bologna."

She went back to take a bite.

"I love bologna." He had a slightly wanton look.

She made a face, put the half back on the plate, held it out to him. "Here, you take it."

"No! It's your sandwich! You eat it. Is there any more left?"

"No. We're out of everything."

Dave looked almost crestfallen.

"Look, just take the sandwich. I'll get something later."

"No. I'm fine."

She sighed, shrugged, and picked up half to take a bite.

"You're really going to eat that without giving me half?"

She gave him a wry look, reached down, and held out the other half. Dave grabbed it and gobbled it down before Samantha even took one bite. She stared at him in awe.

"Too much mustard."

Coma

The relatives stood around her hospital room. There were four of them: Two nieces, a brother and his wife. Even the younger niece was in her fifties. The stroke had been massive. Brain death. She was breathing on her own, but her eyes were closed, and they were staying that way. "There's always hope," the doctor had said, which meant there's no hope.

That was how they understood it, anyway.

"Should I call to make the arrangements?" her brother asked, taking charge, as men will do.

"For the funeral?" the older niece asked, more matter-of-fact than surprised.

"Yeah, I think it would be good to get that started."

The other niece nodded.

His wife, sitting in the chair, her chubby frame squeezed into a dress at least one size too small, asked, "What should we serve?" She looked up at her husband. "I assume we'll come back to our house after the funeral."

The younger niece's eye caught a sparkle of light downstream of the florescent tube planted on the ceiling above. She turned her head to her aunt's face. The younger woman's eyes widened and her mouth opened. She saw it, and she lifted her hand to quiet the others.

They followed her look to the bed, and they all saw it: The old woman's face, still sallow and without expression, her head on the flat hospital pillow, with a lone tear rolled down the outer corner of her left eye, still closed.

The Cross

She expected it, but she was still excited to be maid of honor. It was her best friend's wedding. She bought a special dress.

She didn't like the groom: He was cold and didn't like Jews. But she wasn't the one marrying him, so she didn't care. It was the priest who caused the problem.

It would be sacrilege to have her up there on the podium after what her people had done to the Lord, he said. It was 1956, and he stood his ground. The groom stood with him. How could her friend fight, fight them both—her husband-to-be and her priest?

So her friend told them she understood. They would allow her to stand in the back of the church and watch from there. Her friend pleaded with her, so she let it go and agreed, regretting it almost immediately.

As she stood in the back watching them, backs to her, on their knees, priest over them, her eyes fixed on the crucifix hanging high overhead, in the most honored position, looming over them all.

She looked at him, there on the cross, his face bearded and ragged, head drooping in his misery, body hanging from those nails. Her eyes went up to the letters on the sign atop the cross: INRI, which, she knew, was the Latin abbreviation for "Jesus of Nazareth, King of the Jews."

She looked back down at the priest, who finished his benediction, never seeing her face.

Fuck You, You Fucking Fucks! and Other Tales of Old New York

He had that look on his face, half-bedraggled and half-amused.

"How you doing?" I asked. He was one of my favorite co-workers, down-to-earth and friendly, with a great sense of irony.

"The cops were out this morning, booting cars." He gestured in a sweeping motion. "Up and down the street, every car with overdue tickets." He smirked, approving and disapproving at the same time. "People were throwing garbage on them out their windows, yelling at them." He was Puerto Rican with a pencil moustache that turned up with that smirk, and he continued, shaking his head.

"People were just screaming at them, 'Fuck you, you fucking fucks!'"

I laughed and looked at him, "That's what you get for living in the Bronx."

He shrugged his shoulders. "It sucks, but what can they do? They gotta keep the animals in line."

I hated the job but loved the stories, always perched on the edge, between tragedy and comedy, like the co-worker who got fired for billing three clients for his time while he was on vacation in the Caribbean or that time another co-worker's cat fell off the roof of his apartment building and ended up in a body cast.

"I think he was pushed," I said.

"Nah. He jumped," said someone else.

I still remember visiting him at the pet hospital on East 86th Street, before they put him down.

The job ended too, not long after that, and I moved. The City's changed, I'm sure, but the stories remain.

Farting in an Elevator while Pregnant

It wasn't crowded—only three people—so she stepped on. They gave her room. She reached for the panel, and the man in the corner reached up. "What floor?"

"Three," she said.

The doors closed, and the elevator moved oh-so-slowly. She needed a toilet, and this was the nearest building. She picked three, because it was the lowest floor that was guaranteed to have a bathroom. Besides, it was her lucky number.

But what if it needed a key? Or the janitor was cleaning it? Her mind raced.

She was due in nine days, and the ligaments in her pelvis were killing her. She was hungry and about to pee in her pants. Then she felt it—her stomach grumbling. Nothing to worry about. Just that Mexican lunch that she inhaled an hour ago.

The elevator stopped on two, and she thought she was going to burst. Another man got on. She moved to make room, and it slipped out. She saw the man by the panel smirk and the lady to her left roll her eyes and look away.

"I'm pregnant," she said.

"I know," said the man behind her.

I'm about to give birth to a three-pound burrito! She thought.

The doors opened, and there was the bathroom. Someone was coming out and held the door for her, key dangling from her hand.

It just had a single toilet, but it was private and clean. *Lucky three,* she thought, as she sat relieving herself and caressing her belly.

The Poem

He held the paper and read from it carefully, with just a hint of mischief. "Tomorrow's yesterday is today, and yesterday's tomorrow is today; but the day after tomorrow's yesterday is tomorrow, and the day before yesterday's tomorrow is yesterday."

She looked at him. "You're an idiot."

Faux-insulted, he protested. "I thought it was good!"

"That is not a poem," she replied.

"Yes it is!"

"I don't know what it is." She looked at him. "You probably plagiarized it." Then she thought for a second. "No, it's not good enough. You probably just got it off the internet."

He turned red. Bingo.

She shook her head. "Don't worry, I'll help you."

He breathed out. "But Mrs. Himmelfarb'll know you wrote it."

She knitted her eyebrows, annoyed. "I didn't say I was going to write it for you."

"Oh," he said, part puzzled and part disappointed.

Of course, she knew she was going to end up writing it for him, but at least she'd make him sweat for it.

"Are you hungry?"

"Yeah, I'm starving."

"I'll make some oatmeal."

"With peaches?"

"Yeah, with peaches."

"Is that a poem?"

She smirked a little. She knew what he meant: the back-and-forth between them—could he write it down and call it a poem—but she decided to take it the other way, about the oatmeal itself. "It's poetry the way I make it."

He smiled and laughed, and she smiled back as she got out the saucepan. Can't work on an empty stomach.

Aspergum Junkie

You wore glasses that were too big for your face. Real flying saucers. With convex lenses that bent the light around your head in a way that made it look like it was being squeezed in half by a giant rubber band.

Even so, you were pretty.

You sat in the back of your math class, in your black pants, legs spread apart like a boy, imagining a sick day at home with your mother, chewing Aspergum and watching Tom and Jerry.

You were almost sixteen, but your mother still kept the gum.

"It's good for sore throats," she'd say.

She thought it was the orange Tang taste you loved so much, but really it just reminded you of the small woman with the brilliant blue eyes.

You would see those eyes and taste that orange gum, even as your figure grew long and slender and your glasses shrank, and you gave blankets to your own little girl, curled up, on a sick day far in the future, with that same sparkling look.

Bridge and Tunnel

She had big hair and tight jeans. Her eyes were blue, but she looked ethnic: Jewish or Italian but not Irish and not Protestant. So did her friends, who were dressed the same but not as pretty. Three girls, out on the town, coming off the R or the N train from Brooklyn or Queens or maybe the tube from Jersey.

They'd window shop but never buy, go to a club but not a movie, eat but never dine.

Their ancestors had escaped the jungle of the Lower East Side for the wilds across the treacherous waters, now connected by man-made arteries, pumping people in one direction, then the other.

They'd have their day: Walking and laughing, searching for a clean bathroom and a place to eat, looking at other tight jeans, turning some heads. Then they'd go back down underground and cross back through the divide.

She'd replay the conversations and think about the day as it slipped into night, the sky darkening, under clean sheets, the reality dissolving into dreams of the island on the other side.

Friends

Happily drunk, she fell asleep. It was the top floor of the frat house, the furthest room down on the left. No one was supposed to be there. She had hardly closed her eyes when she felt it. Hands, on her body, touching her. She scrambled up, in a panic, suddenly awake, banging her hand on the way to the light switch. It was Jimmy, laughing his ass off. Her hand was throbbing.

"You're such an asshole," she said, relieved, but still annoyed. He seemed to always be having fun at her expense.

"You know I love you," he said still laughing.

"Then let me sleep," she said.

He did. Even as he did, he watched her. And he dreamt of picking his chest hairs off of her breasts.

Pallbearer

It was the weight that jarred me. I wasn't expecting it. She shuffled in her cocoon, and I shuddered at the thought of dropping her. We didn't, even as we lowered her for her final wait to be covered in that blanket of dirt. I read a poem and a prayer.

After, we ate and went to the Go-Kart track to ride the cars. Still in our black suits and white shirts and tailored dresses, we flexed our muscles and sped around the curves of the oval. We laughed and smiled, wistful and pointed, glad to be alive, bumping tires and skidding through the backstretch. We ate a final meal, and then it was really over. Later, back home, I saw the black flecks of track and rubber on my white shirt. I smiled as I picked them off.

The Purple Skoda of Prague

Nobody knows, but the Golem of Prague lives in a purple 1961 Skoda Felicia. I met him when I went there on vacation. He grinned at me through his chrome grill, before I stepped in and took my seat, waiting for him to take me around the city.

I saw the bridge across the Vltava River through his open roof, and the great castle of Prague, the artisan's clock still beating its mechanical heart, the Charles University, split into German and Czech halves, where Einstein taught and wrote his theories before leaving the city for another appointment. And the long hallways of the official buildings that planted themselves in Kafka's mind.

The car bucked when we passed the Altneuschul, his old home, the place where he was born, and I knew. The tour guide, who owned the car, pointed it out from the driver's seat, just as he pointed out all of the other sites, but he had no clue.

When the tour was done, and we were back where we started, I got out of the car and noticed that the 'S' was missing from the front of the hood, leaving 'koda.' I asked about it and what "Skoda" meant, and the tour guide told me that it meant "damage" or "harm."

"I've looked, but it's an old car, and I can't find a new letter," he told me.

"That's okay," I said. "I like it the way it is."

He shrugged, but the Felicia just sat and grinned.

City Island

I used to get fried clams at the place down at the end of City Island. I'd eat and watch the seagulls circling off the water, scavenging leftovers in the salt breeze.

"It almost makes you forget it's the Bronx," I told my date one time.

"It's different up here, the river," an old timer chimed in.

"What do you mean?" my date asked.

"The East River, it's cleaner," I explained.

"That's not what I mean," he said. "It's wider, more open." He pointed with his hand to the inlets across the water. "With those deep cuts from the glacier, when it came down, last ice age."

Turns out, he was a professor at the Maritime College, PhD from Columbia School of Mines, taught deep-sea mining for thirty years.

It didn't work out with the date. In fact, I never saw her again. But I'd go up and meet the professor: when I could, at first, then every Wednesday after work in the summers, and every Saturday, regardless, until he died.

We'd talk about the tides and the currents, all the old shipwrecks, mining the East River, and sunken treasure. "It's all down there," he told me. "Silver ingots, gold coins, but you'll never bring it up. Two inches of visibility; some of the fastest water in the world."

We went out on the water once. It was the last time. I met his children that day. I can still see the weighted body slipping out from under the flag.

Pirates

When I was ten years old, my father took me to Forbes Field for the first time. Walking up the tunnel to our seats, the live field flowed into my eyes. It was so green, it nearly blinded me.

He and my older brothers would still talk about Bill Mazeroski and that home run over the left field wall that beat the Yankees in the 1960 World Series.

Years later, when he was dying from Alzheimer's and didn't even recognize my mother, he still remembered that ball sailing over the left field wall. When I'd pull out that black and gold cap, he'd smile a proud little grin and say "Pirates."

He's dead now. So is Mazeroski. They tore the old ballpark down and the one that came after it, too long ago to remember.

The Girl in the Green Velvet Dress

She stood, one foot propped up, leaning against the wall, dark stockings and velvet dress, the color of money.

She surveyed the room, with her Mona Lisa smile, and he imagined that she was Daphne and that he, struck dumb by her beauty, was Phoebus Apollo, Golden Greek, streaking through the sky, chasing her in his chariot.

Watching her from the corner of his eye, he imagined her laugh, as she stood, still as a laurel tree.

Opposites

He went through a phase where he only ate combinations of foods whose names were opposites: Orange roughy with a banana smoothie, white rice with black beans, angel hair pasta with Devil's Food cake.

His mother indulged him. What else could she do?

He was idiosyncratic but good-natured. He cried when he saw a dead pigeon and laughed when his brother farted. He didn't generally get good grades, until he solved a problem in math class that even the teacher couldn't figure out.

When he went off to college, his mother wanted to go with him. Her heart ached, but she never betrayed it.

He was popular with the girls in school, even though they were in short supply at the technical university where he went, and he got married to one of them right after graduation, a stunning beauty with a kind heart.

He had a boy of his own after a while.

"He won't eat fish," his wife complained to him one night.

He saw the banana smoothie on the table, still a favorite. "Get some orange roughy next time," he said. "It's a great combination."

She furled her eyebrows, but the boy got it, chuckled and nodded. That should do the trick—a family tradition.

The Tuchis Monster

His aunt had a huge butt—the kind that made it difficult to get into an airplane seat or sit on a barstool. She wasn't fat; it was just her bottom that was big.

One time, she was looking for a recipe that she'd misplaced. His baby brother saw it when she got up. Not on the couch where she was just sitting but stuck up her crack, those oversized cheeks having closed around it, partially swallowing it when she stood.

"Look! The Tuchis Monster ate it!" he yelled from his high chair, pointing at the paper in the groove of her slacks.

He and his brother couldn't stop laughing, and whenever something got lost after that, they'd say that the Tuchis Monster ate it.

She took it in stride. She never had children of her own and ended up paying for both boys to go to college. He went to medical school afterwards, and his brother became a lawyer. She paid for that too.

Years later, when she was dying, he took care of her. Her mind was still sharp, and she joked about her butt being too big for the bedpan.

"Don't want the Tuchis Monster to eat it," she said, winking at him.

He turned red but smiled. "Now you're just being cheeky."

She laughed, even though he could see she was in pain. It was the last time he saw her.

The Tuchis Monster gets us all in the end, he thought. She'd like that one.

Amores

He loved her smile, the gap between her teeth, the way she filled out her skirt. He loved how she jiggled when she wrote on the board. He loved her.

He sat in front to better see—such a dramatic improvement over the man who'd taught Latin the year before.

Whenever she asked a question, he'd shoot up his hand. If he got it, he'd get to see her smile; if not, he'd have an excuse to see her after class.

She was kind, smelled good, and loved poetry.

He knew she was married, that the other boys thought she was frumpy, but he also knew that her husband was the luckiest man in the world.

At year's end, she gave him her volume of Ovid. He wanted to tell her that he loved her, but he knew not to.

Early one evening at the supermarket, years later, he saw a woman, just his type, carefully selecting apples. She turned around, noticed him looking, and smiled. It was her.

She had some gray and a few wrinkles but was still beautiful. He had a girlfriend but wondered if she was still married as they talked.

A little boy flew up and wrapped his arms around her waist.

"I have to go," she said, dropping a third Golden Delicious in her bag. "It was wonderful to see you."

"Hic, poma dulcia sunt,"[1] he blurted out, not wanting her to leave.

She grinned, reached out, hugged him, then kissed his cheek.

"Indeed."

---

[1] "Here, the apples are sweet."

Blueberries for Salvatore

Whenever they went to Vermont, he felt like he was in witness protection. "That's what happens when you're from Jersey," he'd say.

He was going to write a children's book about it, for kids who wanted to be mobsters: *Blueberries for Salvatore*. There'd be a shakedown for more blueberries and collection money, paid in blueberries; brown paper bags, filled to the brim. "Those are some nice looking berries. Wouldn't want to see anything happen to them."

His wife thought it was funny at first, but then she realized he was serious.

"That's the worst idea I've ever heard."

"What do you know? You're from up here. In witness protection land. This'll be huge in Jersey. Huge."

"So you want to turn a beautiful children's story into The Godfather for budding young thugs?"

He took it in. "Well, I wouldn't put it that way."

"What about the bears? There were bears in the original." She had him.

"I thought of that. The mother bear is a hit man. The cub is his associate."

So she let him run with it.

It was when he started to do the drawings that she realized something was wrong.

"Blueberries are supposed to be blue," she told him.

"They are blue," he said.

It turned out he had a lesion on his frontal lobe. It was benign, and it had probably been there for years.

"Leave it," the doctor said. "If you can put up with the quirks."

Protection money, she thought. And she nodded.

Pass / Fail

You should be back at your dorm in Manhattan, studying for your O-Chem final, but you're at a bar in East New York, Brooklyn, talking to a woman—long legs, short skirt. You're pretty sure she's a hooker.

You go to her place. It turns out she's not a pro after all. Just a wannabe actress, current waitress, with a lonely heart and deep eyes. Half Ethiopian, half Syrian. Her smile makes you forget about that exam, but you can't. You get her number and head out.

It's later than you realized, and the streets are nearly deserted. You walk to the C train at Van Siclen Avenue, but you get a bad feeling and catch a Gypsy cab instead.

The driver's from Albania, and his name has more consonants than the leftovers from a game of scrabble. You notice he's going in the wrong direction, and he tells you he has to see his mother in Queens. You protest, but he barely speaks English and shrugs his shoulders like he doesn't understand.

He stops at a small house in Woodhaven. You know the subway is nearby—the C train at Lefferts Boulevard—and you pay him and bail out.

You've got no money left and jump the turnstile.

You get back, cram for the exam, and sleep for an hour.

You end up with a B+ but decide not to apply to medical school after all.

You call the girl with the deep eyes, but the number's been disconnected.

The Violin Maker

They saw her through the window at the side of the Vienna Opera House, articulating pieces together with delicate movements, gestating a new instrument into existence.

It was already recognizable, and they were both mesmerized by the creation.

She caught them looking and was surprised but not pleasantly, her privacy shattered. The woman smiled, but the violin maker waved her off, appearing to almost fear the attention.

"I can understand," the man said, as they walked off. "I'm sure she feels like a monkey at the zoo."

But still, they wanted to know, to know how such beauty came into the world, and they resented her unwillingness to show them. They talked about it for a while, wondering how she came to be a violin maker, why she was working by a window in a busy area, if she even knew how to play the instruments that she created.

Then they forgot about her, as they toured the sites of Vienna: The many apartments where Beethoven, the consummate artist—and terrible tenant—had lived; the house where Schubert died; the golden statue of Johann Strauss.

It was when they came across a shop selling used instruments, with an antique violin in the front window, that they spoke of her again. It was beautiful, and they wondered, ominously, who the former owner was, who had made it, and what had happened to them.

"We'll never know," he said, as they admired the violin, so fragile and so robust, through the window.

Peace on Earth
or That Time I Made My Fourth Grade
Music Teacher Cry

She was twenty-four, blonde, with blue eyes, pale skin, and features that looked like they were molded from a tomb at Westminster Abbey.

She was earnest to a fault, precise in her motions, and exacting in her standards.

She led the choir at chapel. I still remember the hymns.

She used Ms., and taught us the song, "One Tin Soldier."

So we sang about the people from the valley who massacred the mountain people for the treasure hidden under a rock, which is revealed, in the end, to be nothing more than a message: ". . . and peace on earth was all it said!"

It was ridiculous.

How could they let themselves be killed for a nonexistent treasure? They could have just told them the message!

I knew people with numbers on their arms. I remembered the Munich Massacre from the year before. The Yom Kippur War had just ended.

I was in no mood for the drumbeat of Christian martyrdom.

So I mocked it. Mercilessly. And nothing she did could get me to stop. Until finally, her tears began to flow. Anger. Frustration. And a visit to the headmaster's office.

He was a good man. He liked his Scotch but not to excess and played the trumpet, like I did. I'm not sure that he exactly understood, but he had a boys-will-be-boys attitude, told me to behave, or there would have to be consequences, and sent me back to class.

So I did. And Peace on Earth was all it said.

The Yearbook

The class of 1938, they were all in it. Suits and ties, in black and white. Contented faces, soon to have their Ivy League degrees in hand, awaiting life's bounty.

As I flipped through the pages, I saw notes written, some in pencil, some in ink, beside many—though not all—of the graduating seniors. *Killed in action, Tarawa, 11/21/43; Died, car accident, Stonington, Connecticut, July 7, 1938; Died, cancer, New York City, 10/7/1980.*

There was no name in the yearbook. It was just a random find in a used bookstore in New England. I bought it for five dollars. There was a Russian prince—the scion of a noble family chased from his homeland by the Red

Revolution. There were future captains of industry, future fathers, uncles, and professors. And people who did not have long to live or were otherwise destined for failure and tragedy. Some lived to be over a hundred; some died not long after graduation.

Man plans and God laughs, I thought.

There is a story about a man who knows the exact time and circumstances of his death. It's unbearable, a living hell. Maybe even a sort of living death.

People often bemoan the caprice of life, but it guides our destiny. I see it in those faces, a moment in time in an infinite spectrum, a spectrum of possibilities. A good bargain, I figure.

Closed Casket

There wasn't a straight panel left on the car, including the side that wasn't hit. Even the ashtray was knocked loose. Blown red light, T-boned by a truck. Five girls out for the evening—their last. A sudden end. All gone.

He got the call just after midnight and sent for his crew to do the cleanup. They met at the intersection of the crash.

It was a mess. Debris everywhere. Blood, darkening; tissue, white matter, thickening and drying.

Two of them were thrown clear; three still in the car. The driver, pinned in her seat; another in the back; the last one turned upside down, on top of her—her skirt pushed up towards her waist; her underwear, showing.

"Can we cover her up?" he asked the cop in charge.

"Yeah, of course. We were waiting for the coroner," he said, attempting to excuse the oversight.

Another cop put a blanket over her.

He had a smoke with one of his guys and that cop in charge, when the coroner finally showed up and took care of business.

He never got used to those thick black body bags.

The flatbed came and hauled off the car. He hadn't noticed before, but every window was shattered too.

The cleanup was easy and anticlimactic. Sometimes it was like that.

At home, he kept thinking of the girl in the back seat and had the urge to go to her funeral, but he didn't.

He never did.

Reading Dynamics

Every week, he and his old man would head into the City. It was 1975, and New York was festering with graffitied subways and muggings.

The class was in a pre-war building in midtown. Fluorescent lights and white linoleum floors offset the rundown, out-of-date interior. The classroom was long and narrow with industrial carpet, looking like a repurposed storage room. They sat in the back.

The teacher was a dentist. The class, Speed Reading Dynamics. It was all the rage.

He was the only kid but had no trouble. Not so the fellow in front. He was about twenty-five, and, it became clear, couldn't read. The teacher picked on him.

One day, he'd had enough. He erupted, yelling, blaming the dentist for his inability to understand. And for picking on him. The dentist was taken aback and apologized. The class continued.

Until he jumped up and dropped the dentist with one punch. Everyone froze. Except the old man, who made a beeline to the front.

The dentist was on his back, his assailant looming over. The old man locked eyes with him.

Without fear, he knelt down. "Are you alright?"

"I think so."

The student-turned-boxer hesitated then bolted.

The police arrested him.

The course eventually faced accusations of being a scam, playing on people's panicked need to get ahead, or at least not be left behind.

He still uses it, occasionally, to skim a book or article. It's good for that. But you have to know how to read first.

Dammit Janet

They had their own house on campus, complete with sundry friends and lovers.

Seven a.m. one Saturday, Brit entered the kitchenette in her bathrobe, Andy following in boxers. Jack stood in street clothes, eating a sandwich.

"I had sex with Janet."

Brit's face lit up. "Are you kidding?!"

Andy sat, grinning. "No way!"

Brit flipped on the coffeemaker. "Well congratulations." She sat on Andy's lap. "She's very pretty."

"Totally!" said Andy. "So is she your girlfriend now?"

"I don't know."

"What's up with her arm anyway?" Andy asked.

"The doctor messed it up when she was born."

"That sucks," Andy said.

"As long as it doesn't bother you," Brit added.

He actually hadn't thought about it until then.

"You should call her," Brit told him.

"Why?"

"To see how she's feeling!" She got up and poured. "Do you want her to be your girlfriend?"

He shrugged.

She brought coffee over to Andy, sitting back on his lap. "You should call anyway." She looked at him. "How well do you know her?"

"Pretty well."

"Which arm?"

He closed his eyes. "Her right."

"What color are her eyes?"

He hesitated.

"Brown!" Andy blurted out.

"No helping!"

"No, that's not right," Jack said. "They're like yours."

"Hazel?"

"Yeah."

He decided he did want her. More than anything. He went to see her and told her.

She squeezed his hand and looked at him with big, open irises. "I love you. As a friend. But I don't want to date you."

He already knew.

We Hardly Knew Ye

Sometimes the only thing left to give your child is a decent funeral. It'd been three months. My soul throbbed.

We came back from happy hour, a couple of drinks down. A black Escalade was leaving our building. Then, a bunch of blue jackets with big yellow letters: FBI. On our hall, even more commotion. I glanced in the open door opposite ours, home to an elderly couple, swarming with more agents.

"Grandson cooking meth?" I asked.

"Turn on the TV."

An hour later, lead story, Ten O'Clock News. Number one on the Most Wanted List. $800,000 stuffed in the walls; guns hidden in books, their pages cut out to accommodate them. They had new names and always paid the rent in cash.

"Charlie" took an afternoon nap everyday, leaving a "Do not disturb" sign outside their door. He had done time at Alcatraz, was released, and killed nineteen people as crime boss in Boston. Then he vanished. It was her hairdresser that was their undoing.

So there I was, still licking my wounds, being interviewed by *The New York Times, Wall Street Journal,* and *The Boston Globe.* And the FBI.

I found out he had a son who died at six. It was some kind of cosmic nexus.

It's all a blur. Except his hands. They were big, like they could break a man's neck. I remember seeing them reaching for his doorknob, passing him in the hall. Safe haven. But not for long.

The Cosmos is full of surprises.

Pigs in a Blanket

I never liked the term "Pigs in a Blanket." "Cocktail Franks" seems so much more dignified. Not the namesake of a maligned farm animal; but honest and straightforward and not "covered up."

The first time I had them was at my grandmother's retirement party when I was four. I can still remember reaching up to dip them into the mustard, bright yellow, the only way it came back then.

My grandmother was a nurse, head of the night shift, and she needed to step down to take care of my grandfather. She had just passed sixty-five anyway, but I'm sure she would have kept going another few years.

I remember the fluorescent hospital lights and the linoleum-tiled floors in the reception room, almost white but with barely discernable designs, cloudlike, half-hearted, in institutional shades that conveyed a no-nonsense tone. And the wheelchair ramp—endless fun for a small kid. Her supervisor, a woman named Honey, doted on me, as she usually did.

They say all romances end badly. My grandfather died, and my grandmother was alone. Then she died too. And eventually my parents.

I still have the tape recorder she gave me, and sometimes I listen to her voice.

I'm the one on the hospital board now, and they had a reception in the very same room. And I saw them, a whole tray. A kid asked the server what they were, and he told her, *"Saucisses en croûte."*

Pigs in a blanket have come a long way.

Dead for a Long, Long Time

He got a call once. They'd found a body out in the woods. It'd been partially preserved by the moss and moisture. They couldn't even tell the sex at first, but whoever it was, they'd been dead for a long, long time. A jogger, he found out later, a middle-aged man, father of three, out for a morning run. Heart attack. Never came home. Never found. Until he was. Another closed casket.

It was a good job, a public service. He'd made a bunch of friends; a few close ones, and one very nice woman at the coroner's office. He wanted to marry her, but she said no. She was ten years older than he and wore cat's eye glasses and snug white dresses that were in fashion in those days.

He left the job after that and opened a fast food franchise. He married someone else and had three kids of his own. He used to go for morning jogs out in the woods, but he always left his wife a map.

Meeting Mary Poppins

She saw the ad in the newspaper: "Meet Mary Poppins!"

"Julie Andrews is coming to Orlando," she told her daughter-in-law. "We should take the kids."

She had gone to see the original film with her own daughter, now long-dead, many years before.

Jennifer thought it was a great idea. The kids loved the movie. It was close enough to do in one day without having to stop somewhere overnight. She planned it out. She would go up with Linda, spend the day, be home by nightfall. It was just the two of them, widows, one young, the other old. And two small children.

The kids were excited, but something was off. Jennifer hadn't heard anything else about it, and Linda couldn't find the newspaper. She was becoming forgetful—Jennifer could see the beginnings of it—but she dismissed it.

It was a Sunday. They drove up, and Jennifer was surprised to see that the address was a small bookstore. They were the only ones who came for the event. And, indeed, there was Mary Poppins, young and pretty, dressed just like the character in the 1964 movie, and she realized. But she never let on.

She looked over at her mother-in-law, expecting embarrassment, but there wasn't any. Only the wistful joy of the connection to her lost daughter.

The young lady talked to the children, signed their autograph books, and gave them each a hug. They were elated.

"We met Mary Poppins!" the little one exclaimed. And so they had.

The Smell of the Desert

It was a Christmas gig, build a spreadsheet. ASAP. Couldn't wait until after the holiday.

They paid Sam twice his regular rate, for the whole week, even though it would only take him a few hours. They didn't care. "Just show up and get it done." It was at the far end of Wall Street, in a back room with another guy, Rahim, young like him, a techie, studying for his IT certification.

By mid-afternoon, they were shooting the breeze. Maybe it was the Christmas spirit, though neither of them was Christian.

"When I pass my test, I want to be a consultant, make some real money," Rahim said. Brooklyn-born, his family was from Yemen. He had studied computer science at Brooklyn College and was looking to live the American Dream.

His parents didn't like it. So they sent him to a madrassa in Yemen "to be like your cousin." It didn't take. He came back. Things were tense.

"I'll get my certification, get married, move out."

There was a lull in the conversation, and Sam looked out the tiny window. Rain broke the silence, and suddenly they were talking about the smell of rain on the desert, thirsty-wet, musty, like a bone-dry rag taking in all the moisture it can.

They looked at each other in a moment of primeval bonding between people of the desert.

Then it was time to go. They walked out together.

"Merry Christmas," Sam said, grinning, when they parted for the last time.

Kamikaze

What surprised him most was the way the steel turned white hot when it buckled. The shock propagated out like a wave over the ship's deck, throwing him out of his shoes and into the water.

The impact was loud and deliberate. The explosions that came after seemed ancillary, but they took the ship down. He saw it all, smelling the gasoline on the water, watching men burn. June 18, 1945. The day his carrier went to the bottom of the Pacific.

It was less than an hour before a destroyer picked him up, but it seemed like forever. He was reassigned stateside, met a pretty nurse, and married her two months after VJ

Day. He got a business degree on the GI Bill, became a stock broker, and moved to New York.

He was still working into his seventies with four grown children and six grandchildren. He never talked about that day on the carrier and didn't think about it much anymore.

Then he had a dream. He was going to work at the World Trade Center one clear blue day in September. Then that same thud, loud and deliberate. And that white-hot wave. A dream that was reality.

This time on solid ground with his shoes on, he knew the clock was ticking. He was one of the first telling people and helping them to get out.

"But how did you know, Grampa?"

And he told them about that other day, so long ago, out on the Pacific.

Wrinkles

Rima watched her from across the cafe. She'd seen her before, sitting and smoking, legs crossed. Sometimes she drank coffee, always black and always in a ceramic cup. She was never without a cigarette.

She was old and reminded Rima of her grandmother, now dead, chain-smoking alone and stewing in her thoughts.

Smoke stretched into the air, the stream filling the deep ravines in her face. Rima tried to decipher the pattern of wrinkles, as the woman inhaled, paused, and exhaled slowly, with satisfaction that bordered on revenge.

She knew that Arab men didn't let Arab women come to the cafe to smoke their hookahs with them. So her grandmother sat home and smoked alone, even long after her husband was in the ground.

Without warning, the old woman turned and looked at her and let out a little smile, and Rima suddenly saw her grandmother's face and Arabic script in her pattern of wrinkles. She was too stunned to smile back, and the woman looked away.

Rima grabbed her backpack and headed out.

She was modern, wore jeans, went to college, and studied biology. But her parents insisted on arranging her marriage.

She was surprised when the matchmaker produced a fellow student, tall and handsome, who took her breath away.

They agreed to marry.

"One thing I want in the wedding contract—you won't ever go to the cafe to smoke a hookah without inviting me."

He nodded in ascent then smiled. "No problem. Just a minor wrinkle."

Marian, the Librarian

She came in to cool off. The library was air-conditioned. She picked up *Elle* and sat in the back.

When she needed the bathroom, she asked the woman with the oval glasses.

"It's only for staff." She smiled at her. "You have such beautiful eyes."

"Thanks," she said, without smiling back.

"What color are they?"

"My mother says they're cinnamon."

"Well, Miss Cinnamon Eyes, just for you." And she led her through the office to the staff bathroom.

She thanked her. "I'm Jessica."

"I'm Marian."

"Marian the librarian?"

Marian nodded and grinned.

They both laughed, and Jessica smiled for the first time. "I loved *The Music Man!*"

She came in every day after that. She had felt that urge before but ignored it. This time, she let herself go. She was thirty-three, her Jesus year, coming off a bad breakup with a man she'd met in college, and she was in no mood to dive back in with another one.

It turned out Marian was fifty-eight. She was fantastic, with crystal blue eyes and a radiant smile. She wore granny panties and dresses in the summer, and Jessica was crazy about her.

She was ready to quit her job and move up there. Then summer ended, the romance with it. She was crushed.

She returned to the City and never gave in to that urge again. But she thought of Marian often, whenever she went to the library on a hot summer day, whistling that tune from *The Music Man.*

L.A. Story

I went out with an actress when I lived in LA. She was fun and wacky and pretty. She gave me a link to her one-woman show that she wanted me to watch. But I never got around to it. Then we broke up.

I ran into her on the street about a year later, and we started up all over again.

I finally watched her show. She had great stage presence, had the audience eating out of her hand. They were smiling and laughing, on the edge of their seats. Then she told them. And me. She'd had a breakdown, went to a mental institution. She let it out in fits and flashes, how reality went sideways then overtook her and engulfed her and how she found her way back out, but never completely.

"I saw your one-woman show."

She beamed. "What did you think?"

"So, you had your deck shuffled, huh?"

"Yeah." Still beaming with those sparkling eyes, inviting me in for more.

So I dove inside her and saw it all.

Death, abuse, family strife. The good, the bad, and the ugly.

She was a conduit. But there was too much light, and I had to get out. So I did.

I saw her on TV a while later. She played an actress in L.A. who was fun and wacky and pretty. I checked to see if the link was still there, but it was gone.

Green Mountains

He was professor of Hebrew at a Vermont college, married to a woman who was blind and thus the best of listeners. She was the one who noticed.

"There's a pattern to the sound shifts."

No one had seen it before. He extrapolated the meaning of an Akkadian inscription of the late Babylonian Empire and won a fellowship to do research in the Middle East.

They went and experienced the smells of the bazaar and sounds of the languages still spoken there.

They met the Coptic prelate in Cairo and a Yemenite rabbi in Jerusalem.

"They still pronounce the *ayin,*" she said, referring to the guttural Semitic consonant, lost in modern Hebrew; her smile giving him indescribable pleasure.

He told her how the Golan Heights looked like the Green Mountains of Vermont, leaving out the minefields and burned-out Syrian tanks with Arabic script proclaiming their war heroes.

"It smells different," she told him.

"How?"

"Gunpowder. And shells."

They went on a dig in Jordan and made love in the desert.

The men couldn't understand why he married her, even though she was beautiful and fair-skinned, with light eyes and hair. "She's blind and writes with her left hand," a professor from Amman said bluntly, unimpressed by her love of languages and her brilliance.

He got offers after that but returned to the Green Mountains of Vermont.

"I'm pregnant," she told him. And he was glad there was no gunpowder in the air.

She smiled. "I hope he gets your eyes."

Warriors

He was a childhood friend from the neighborhood whose life, now over, took him in the opposite direction. It came on the car radio, and I stopped to listen. They found him in the river; he was dead when he went in.

They wanted him found, I thought, *so his mother could bury him, as a show of respect.*

We'd been out on that river once in a "borrowed" boat—stolen off the piers where he later worked as a longshoreman. It capsized in the wake of a larger ship, and we hung on for dear life. "Don't worry," he told me in a moment of prescience. "This isn't how I'm going." He was half right.

I start the car and continue on my way, losing myself in my thoughts. I see the flowing waters of the Hackensack coddle him, like the River Styx, on his journey to the afterlife. I imagine the sounds of the water, peaceful but relentless, echoing in his now-deaf ears as his body moves downstream through the green, deciduous brush.

I see Lenape tribesmen, fellow warriors, who hunted, fished, and paddled their canoes on this river, standing on its shore, watching in silent tribute.

When I return home, I go to the riverbank to join them and throw a coin in for Charon to ensure his safe passage.

At that moment, I hear the Lenape whisper, and I know that it's all just borrowed. Even our bodies, like the river itself, belong to no one.

The Old Man and the C

She sat on the park bench with her arms spread out, like an eagle. She'd been free of the cancer for ten years and let herself feel that she was done with it forever. An old man walked by and looked right at her chest, protruding prominently. She knew she had nice boobs, and that it looked like she was showing off, but she didn't care. Let him have his free show. He didn't understand, and it didn't matter.

She breathed deeply, relishing that her lungs were clear.

She'd gotten the message just before her lunch break and headed out early. She worked at a call center for a large insurance company. Her friend in the next cubicle would cover.

Funny thing, she wasn't even hungry. She just wanted to be outside in the open air. She just wanted to be.

It had hit her with its best shot, ravaged her body at twenty-six, nearly taken everything. Her fiancé had left her; her mother died shortly after she was diagnosed; and her father two years later. She was already an only child.

After work, her friend took her out for drinks to celebrate. She told her about the old man and how good she felt.

"When was the last time you were on a date?"

"Not since Bill," she said. Then she paused. "Maybe it's time."

"He's probably available," her friend said.

"Who?"

"The old man in the park."

And they looked at each other and laughed.

Long-term Parking

The jewelry box had been on his mother's dresser for as long as he could remember. It was gaudy, but there was something beautiful about it. It had several drawers, and his mother gave him one for his keepsakes: his faux-ruby tie pin; the silver quarter he'd found in their backyard; the last letter from his grandmother before she died.

He asked about it when he got older, and his mother told him. "It was a gift from one of your father's friends, in return for a favor."

He didn't ask which friend or what favor. He never knew his father, but he knew the friends she was talking about and the kinds of favors they did.

Eventually, his mother died, he got married, and the jewelry box went into the attic.

He went to work for his father-in-law, running numbers and collecting debt.

One day, he went to collect the vig off a man who'd gotten in way too deep, and he saw the same jewelry box on his mantle.

"Where'd you get that?"

"My father gave it to my mother," the man told him.

He knew the man's father. They'd found him in long-term parking at JFK, stuffed in the trunk of his Lincoln.

"He gave one to all of his mistresses," the man added, with an inscrutable grin, and he suddenly saw the resemblance, like he was looking in a mirror.

He covered the vig and cancelled the debt—the least he could do for a brother.

The Kids' Table

She was in college, but there she was at the kids' table. A wedding in Brooklyn, at a large Masonic Hall. Friends of her parents. Her sisters got out of it—one had a date; the other was a camp counselor. She knew the guy next to her. He was seventeen—only two years younger than she. He'd grown up since she last saw him.

He made her laugh and took her mind off her troubles. When she went to sit down, he pulled the chair out for her. Looking for the bathroom, they ended up in an empty part of the building.

They sat and talked and he put his hand on hers. They both blushed, and he confessed he'd always had a crush on her. They kissed.

He was a rising senior, and she told him about college.

They went back to the wedding and to their respective lives.

She returned to school in Florida; he ended up in California. They kept in touch—his texts always made her laugh—even as they each married other people.

She found herself back in New York, divorced with two children, when she ran into him on the street. He was widowed with two kids of his own.

When they talked, it was like they had never been apart.

A while later, they got married and had two more children together.

When their oldest was getting married, she asked, "So who's sitting at the kids' table?"

He smirked. "Besides us?"

Cannibals

When the shelling stopped, Lubyanov pushed the dead man off and crawled into the cold blue daylight.

Welcome to Leningrad.

They'd sent him to assess the situation during the Nazi siege and report back to Stalin.

There were bodies in the streets. It was forty below zero, and the ground was too hard to bury them. Finally they used dynamite. The shell holes never seemed deep enough on their own.

He'd heard reports of cannibalism but couldn't confirm them, although he was certain they were true. There were no victims alive to testify; the accused always seemed to have gone insane, laughing madly with their ruddy faces.

He heard Shostakovich's Seventh Symphony, the Leningrad, performed live and liked it but preferred his string quartets.

His real last name was German—Geiger—but he'd changed it long before. To make things worse, he was half-Jewish. But, maybe for these reasons, Stalin trusted him slightly more: He had nowhere to go.

Stalin even asked for his opinion. He told him. "Bargain with the Americans for more Ford trucks, to cross Lake Ladoga on the Road of Life."

They sent him back with an extra ration card, which he thought better than to use.

He expected to be shot when he returned the second time, but he wasn't.

Back in Moscow, he woke up in a cold sweat. But it wasn't Stalin. It was the ruddy faced cannibals laughing madly.

"Go back to sleep, Slava," his wife said.

But he couldn't.

Jewfro

There's something about the theater—people always seem to end up naked together. With their "colleagues." And sometimes their teachers. Maybe it's all the emotion or the sheer unpredictability of the profession.

He'd joined the troupe as an afterthought, when a part he'd tried out for didn't come through, and another part, where he was understudy, was cancelled because the director had a heart attack and the owner sold the venue.

He liked her from the start. They did great scenes together, and the two of them ended up writing the intro and several sketches for the show.

One night, after a performance, they all went out for drinks. The two of them stayed late, and when their legs touched, he took her hand under the table, and she smiled.

He offered her a ride home. She told him she had a roommate, then asked to go to his place. He went flush and then she did too.

When they doffed their clothes, he took her in. She was dark-skinned with a wild head of kinky hair and black coffee eyes. She didn't shave, and the wild nest below matched the one on top.

Afterwards, he watched her walk to the bathroom with those dark, shapely legs and that untamed crop bouncing free.

"Black is beautiful," he blurted out on her return, unsure of his blond, Midwestern self.

She smirked. "Maybe, but you know I'm not black."

"But your hair?!"

She shook her head. "Jewfro."

Paradise on a Razor's Edge

My father committed suicide when I was fourteen. I tried it ten years later. Got in the tub, opened my veins. The super found me, because the pipes leaked and the drip in the basement turned red.

I was in the hospital for two years. That's where I met Danny.

He talked fast, drank espresso, and snacked on Honeycrisp apples. He was energetic and kept no secrets. I heard about his fistula and his girlfriend's bisexual adventures.

He was schizophrenic and smoked unfiltered Luckys, because the nicotine helped.

I moved in with him and Jenny, bought a typewriter at a thrift store, and wrote about the Sargasso Sea. I dreamt of going to Turks and Caicos and asked them to come along.

They did. We got an apartment on the water. I woke one night, forgot where I was, and was glad to be on an island when I remembered.

It was Danny's idea to buy a boat, take to the sea, fish.

We did and made good money, then I got tired. I bought another razor and thought to try again, but the plumbing was leaky, so I let the impulse pass.

Jenny sensed it, took my wrists, and looked at my scars. "Jesus Christ." Then at me. "Aren't you curious?"

"About what's on the other side?"

"No. About what you'd miss for the rest of your life here."

"I hadn't thought about it."

"You should." She paused. "Promise me you will. Promise me you'll stay."

So I promised.

To Live and Die in L.A.

He lived alone in an old Victorian on Alvarado Street in Downtown L.A. He never married, had no children, and no known relatives.

When he died, they descended—the lawyers, the realtors, the museum conservators, even the Historical Society.

He was from an old California family and had artworks from the nineteenth century and documents dating back to when Anglo settlers first arrived, and it was still called Alta California.

Rumor had it that he was part Spanish—maybe even Indian. He never denied it, even when it was unfashionable, despite his blue eyes and pale skin.

They found an original copy of the Treaty of Guadeloupe Hidalgo that ended the Mexican-American War and a letter from President Fillmore when California entered the Union as a free state in 1850.

There was a complete set of 1909 baseball cards from the American Tobacco Company. There were coins and stamps, books and letters.

Then the imposters came, claiming to be long-lost relatives, looking to cash in before the state took everything.

Despite all the treasures, he died without a will.

The lawyer demanded DNA tests, eliminating all but one.

He was thirty, married with children, the product of an old man's dalliance with his housekeeper.

Like the state itself, his profile had it all: Anglo, Spanish, Black, and White.

He ended up giving most of it to the museums and the Historical Society. But he kept the house for his mother.

"I want it to stay in the family," he said.

Bottom of the Harbor

When a train derailed on the trestle across the harbor, he and two others went out in a rowboat to help. The lead cars had already gone under, with the last one, #932, dangling over the edge.

Those waters always seemed to involve life and death: He had almost drowned as a child when some older boys tied him to an ironing board and floated him out on the bay by a rope, only to have him flip face-down as he struggled to get free, until one of them jumped in and saved him. Several years later, he paid it back, diving in to save his brother, who had fallen off the bulkhead.

Third time's a charm, he thought, as they got closer.

Suddenly, the whole chain moved and that third car broke loose and plunged in. The cops and firemen on the bridge scrambled to avoid the swell which quickly reversed and came right at *them* in their tiny boat. They held on as it nearly capsized. But it didn't. The fates are never to be underestimated, and that instant, they smiled.

Most of the bodies were never found. As he closed his eyes that night, he imagined the train on the bottom of the harbor.

He wasn't the only one. People, lots of them, played the numbers—9-3-2.

When it hit, the bookies all went bust, and the FBI came.

The fates, he thought. Then he thought of all those people, somewhere on the bottom of the harbor.

The River God

They all did it. From the five-star generals to the buck privates. Starting with Patton.

It was March, 1945, and the writing was on the wall. The Third Army had just crossed the Rhine at Oppenheim. Patton walked onto the pontoon bridge, whipped it out, and pissed in the father of all German rivers.

Pretty soon, they were all doing it—Churchill, Monty, and every dogface in this man's army, including my old man. He was nineteen.

He said he wasn't scared after that, but I'm not sure I believe it.

The Rhine was a hard line for the Romans. The French didn't fare much better. But the winds blew different this time, and my father ended the war somewhere in the middle of Germany, alive, intact, and victorious. He brought home a Luger and a cup of dirt.

I visited once not long after my father had died.

Most rivers in German are feminine. The Rhine is an exception, the living embodiment of the river god. I knew that child sacrifice had been part of their ancient ritual and thought about that as I stood in the modern country, looking out over the magnificent flow, so vibrant and alive.

I'd heard that Patton procured a bust of Hitler for his dog to piss on, and I thought about the human heart that has such energy, yet so much of it gets spent to keep itself on course. Not so the Rhine. Despite it all, the River God never wavers.

In the Act

"I caught my grandparents screwing."

"Are you kidding me?"

He shook his head.

"Like, what am I supposed to do with that?"

He shrugged, smiled, and laughed a little. "Just thought I'd share."

She glared at him. "This is not putting me in the mood. If you're interested."

His brain almost exploded for the second time that day. They were still in high school, and opportunities were few and far between.

Why did he have to mention his grandparents?!

Despite her repulsion, her curiosity got the best of her. "So, was he on top of her?"

"No, she was on top."

She looked even more horrified than before. "So you saw your grandmother naked?!"

He thought for a second. "Just from behind. Just her back really. And the top of her butt."

They were quiet after that.

His parents were upstairs, and she began to drift off in his arms, eyes closed. "Will you still love me when I'm old?"

"Always."

"Maybe someday we'll have grandkids who forget to knock."

He thought about that after she was asleep, and decided he liked the idea, the idea of always being with her. He imagined her at twenty, thirty, forty . . . as he drifted off to join her in his dreams.

Working Girl

In her baby-blue sweater, she waded through the forest of cubicles into his office. She was forty-one, attractive, and well-put-together.

He was only twenty-seven, but he was her boss. "You're my best sales person." He paused. "I'm in love with you."

He saw her expression. His heart sank.

"I don't feel the same way," she said. She saw the disappointment, exposure, and pain in his face. "I'm sorry."

"It's okay," he said.

"Please don't feel foolish."

"You're the nicest person I've ever met."

She wanted to take his hand but didn't dare. "I have to get back to work," she told him, looking as serious as he'd ever seen her. "But please call me later."

He did.

"I just wanted to make sure you were okay." She started. "I didn't want to leave it like that."

He told her that it was at her birthday party, when she hugged each person so warmly, that he fell for her.

They talked occasionally after that, bonded by his secret, even after they both left the company; even after he got married.

When she died, he came to her funeral. He couldn't believe how many people were there.

She had no family, and her estate couldn't cover the cost of the burial; so he offered to pay, only to discover that several other people had stepped in before him.

He thought of her in her baby-blue sweater, and he smiled.

Water's Edge

The city looked different from the water: bigger and more imposing yet smaller and more distant at the same time.

He came from Barbados, where he dove for sponges, to become a scuba cop in New York's murky waters.

"Diving in the East River, it ain't like diving in the Caribbean," he'd say.

He met Abigail at the Harbormaster's Office. She was chief assistant, and he was assigned to clear underwater obstructions and keep the channels open.

He took her out on his boat, made her dinner, and kissed her under the crescent moon off the lower Brooklyn piers.

They got married and had two children, but they fought over money.

One night, after an argument, he stormed off to the water's edge in a fierce rain. He saw a boat capsized and called the station.

He went in to save them, got them on the police boat, but got caught in the current.

Abigail and his children stood in the rain at the water's edge as he fought to make land.

He wasn't sure if he was dead or alive.

Finally, he climbed over the rocks and collapsed.

He woke up in the hospital. Hypothermia. Exhaustion. But alive. His wife and children were there. Hugs and tears. And a hero's medal.

He became Harbormaster after that, and they didn't fight anymore. When his son wanted to dive, he sent him down to the turquoise waters of Barbados. "Bring back some sponges," he told him. "I could use a bath!"

Key West

She didn't usually wear shorts because of her scar—the after-effect of a college motorcycle accident several years before—but it was August in Key West, and it was hot. He seemed to sense it and caressed her thigh.

They were at dinner, on their honeymoon, and it made them both want to go back to the motel. They'd spent half the day there, a tangle of skin and sweat, starting with the roosters crowing at dawn.

"You've got a lot of energy for an old guy," she teased.

"You're just so damn beautiful," he told her, looking her in the eye, smiling, ready to go again.

He never seemed to notice her scar or any of her flaws.

They'd met at the Fontainebleau in Miami. She worked the front desk; he was poolside bartender.

She'd come after work for a drink and a smoke; he'd give her a ride home, so she didn't have to take the bus.

They fell in love and got married, even though he had children who were older than she was. Even though he did drugs and lived in a basement apartment.

But it got to be too much. The unpaid bills. His lack of ambition.

They ended up getting an annulment, because he was Catholic, which always bothered her.

She went up north and remarried, a real catch.

She was happy, for the most part, but there were cold winter nights where she longed for his touch and the heat of Key West.

Desert Rose

The engine squealed as she pulled into the gas station.

"Belt's going," he told her, looking under the hood.

He didn't work there, but he saw her, hapless under the Arizona sun, parked his motorcycle, and came over.

Her face was blank.

"Fan belt," he added. He pushed under the rubber so she could see the cracks.

"Is that why I'm having trouble starting it?"

"No. Starter's probably shot too."

He talked to the mechanic. She used the toilet, got an iced coffee, and waited for him inside the café.

"It's going to take at least two days to get the parts," he told her.

Then the rumble of another motorcycle. And a man and a woman came in and joined them in the booth. Part of the gang. *His* gang.

He looked at her. "You can stay at my place if you want. Take the bedroom. I'll sleep on the couch."

She was young and looked innocent, but she wasn't. She liked him and was grateful for the offer. "Thanks."

The other biker made a crack about "Bobby's prison tats," so she told them: She'd done a four year stretch and was out less than a year.

She wasn't violent. She slept with the head guard, so he'd protect her.

But it changed everything. *Respect.* She was one of them. Even though she wasn't.

She sold her car and stayed for two years. Then she left. But she still has Bobby's name and a rose tattooed on her bottom.

Coke and Ice

Danny was constantly in trouble in school, so his parents sent him to spend the summer with his older cousin, Jane. "She'll be a good influence," his mother told him.

Somehow it escaped her that Jane was dealing coke with her boyfriend, Rick, slept with a gun under her pillow, and had a $2,000 a week habit of her own.

She had a '72 Capri, with a V6 and a four-speed stick, and they'd tool around town, skimming off the top, the good stuff, right up their noses. She let Danny try out her car, while she and Rick were up in the apartment screwing.

Rick gave her a diamond necklace, even though she really wanted a diamond ring, but she didn't complain.

They all went to Disneyland, when they still used paper tickets, and they did more coke, before the three of them crammed themselves into the Capri and went back to the apartment.

When Danny came home, he seemed more relaxed.

"How was it?" his mother asked, with a note of hope.

He popped a can of Coke, poured it over ice, and took a long drink. Then he looked at her with a satisfied grin. "It was the best summer I ever had."

To see our other great titles,
visit us at:

BLACKBIRD BOOKS
www.bbirdbooks.com

www.ingramcontent.com/pod-product-compliance
Lightning Source LLC
Chambersburg PA
CBHW021239230325
23931CB00029B/266